To Francine and Joseph,
You are always there for me.
— B.P.

For Neve —
May you always be free to be who you are!
— L.M.

Thank you, Marvin, for your beautiful arrangement of
"Stella's Song."
— B.P.

All author royalties from this book will be donated to
a program which promotes the adoption of shelter animals.

Text copyright © 2010 by Bernadette Peters
Illustrations copyright © 2010 by Liz Murphy
Stella's Song music and lyrics copyright © 2010 by Bernadette Peters
All rights reserved / CIP Data is available.
Published in the United States 2010 by
Blue Apple Books, 515 Valley Street, Maplewood, N.J. 07040
www.blueapplebooks.com

Distributed in the U.S. by Chronicle Books
First Edition 03/10
Printed in Shenzhen, China

ISBN: 978-1-60905-008-5

2 4 6 8 10 9 7 5 3 1

Bernadette Peters

STELLA IS A STAR!

paintings by **Liz Murphy**

BLUE APPLE BOOKS

This is the story of Princess Pig —

who really isn't a princess . . . or a pig.

She is, in fact,
a dog named Stella—
a dog who doesn't
think anyone
likes her, so she
masquerades
as a pig princess
of the highest order.

Now, you might ask why
Stella thinks no one
likes her.

Well, Stella has a great big smile,
but when everyone looks at her,
they just see a great big mouth
and cross to the other side
of the street.

Stella really wants
to make friends.
So . . .
she decides to sign up
for lessons at
Madame Cochon's
*If Pigs Could Fly
School of Dance,*
because . . .

a dance class
is the perfect place
to find friends.
And,
as everyone knows,
pigs are
the best dancers.

The next day at Madame Cochon's,
Stella introduces herself.

DANCING SCHOOL

"Welcome,"
says Madame.

"I am Princess Pig."

The other dancers gather around her.

"You smell and sound just like a dog."

"You look like a dog with a great big mouth," says Iris.

"Are you really a pig?" asks Petunia.

"Oh, no!
I am definitely
a pig princess,"
says Princess Pig.
"Look at
my crown!"

"If you're a pig,
where is your
curly tail?"
asks Rose.

"My tail's right here. Look!" Princess Pig answers.

Princess Pig
twirls around
to show off her tail
and . . .

falls flat on her face!

"You can't dance,"
says Rose.

"SILENCE!"

Madame Cochon walks briskly into the room.

"This is a dance class, not a circus. Positions, please!"

Madame taps the floor with her stick.
"From the beginning.

Five ... six ...

seven ... eight.

GO!"

One by one, the dancers twirl across the floor.
Rose is the lead dancer and does thirty-two perfect turns.

"Twirl, twirl, twirl," says Madame.

When it is Princess Pig's turn,
she takes a deep breath, leaps, then trips and falls.

Everyone laughs. Everyone but Madame.

"Try again, my dear. Our recital is soon.
We all must practice, practice, practice.
Remember, practice makes perfect."

Princess Pig does
practice, practice, practice.

She pirouettes at breakfast.

She jetés at lunch.

She pliés at dinner.

But practice doesn't make perfect.

"Will I ever be a real dancer?"
wonders Princess Pig.

At last, it's the big night.

SHOW
TONIGHT

Princess Pig warms up backstage.
She is nervous. Very nervous.

Rose practices her turns.
Faster and faster she spins.

All of a sudden,
there is a "POP!"

She topples to the ground.
"Owww, owww!

I twisted my ankle,"
Rose cries.
"I can't dance, Madame."

"But the show must go on,"
says Madame.
"Who has been practicing,
and can take Rose's place?"

Madame looks at Princess Pig.
"You've become a fine dancer.
It is time for you to move
out of the chorus."

"Me?"
Princess Pig gasps.
"I can't do thirty-two
perfect turns!

I would have to take off
my crown, and then no one
would like me."

Madame Cochon says,
"My dear, why don't you give them a chance?"

The music plays. The show begins.
Princess Pig pulls her crown down
to make sure it's on tight.
She walks to the center of the stage,
takes a deep breath, and . . .
starts to dance.

She does her first and second turns
and begins to tip over.
Her crown is too heavy!

When Princess Pig finishes
her third and fourth turns,
her crown wiggles.

After her
fifth and sixth spins,
it wobbles.

On turns seven and eight,
her crown flies off
and she straightens up.

Princess Pig
feels much lighter
without her crown . . .
just like a pup!

On nine and ten,
she is twirling and twirling.
Eleven and twelve,
whirling and whirling.

Thirteen and fourteen,
a spinning top.

Fifteen and sixteen,
"I don't want to stop!"

Seventeen and eighteen,
a blinding light.

Nineteen and twenty,
Princess Pig actually
takes flight.

From twenty to thirty-two, she flies across the floor.
Princess Pig is feeling as never before.

She is finally herself — a pit bull ballerina,
and everyone loves her in the arena.

Stella can be just who she is:
a dog who loves to dance
and a true-blue friend.
No more Princess Pig,
and no need to pretend.

"FANTASTIQUE!"
says Madame.

Stella looks embarrassed.
"You like me even though
I'm not really a princess? Or a pig?"

"We always knew you weren't a pig,"
says Madame.
"You're a dog. And a dancer. A *real* dancer.
You should be proud."

"I am,
Madame!"

And then Stella dances as Madame sings . . .

Don't be afraid to be who you are,
That's what I want to see.
And don't be afraid to reach for the stars,
If you do, that's where I want to be.

Sometimes a heart can close the door,
That's not what you want to do.
Sometimes a heart needs so much more,
Just open it so love can come through.

Don't be afraid to follow your dream,
You have to let it grow.
And don't be afraid to trust who you are,
So you can be the friend you'd like to know.

I need to know that you are there.
You need to know that we all care.
Don't be afraid, we are all near.
Don't be afraid, we are all here . . . for you.